**Read all the adventures
starring the fact-astic**

CAPTAIN FACT
DINOSAUR ADVENTURE

by
Knife & Packer

VOLO

Hyperion Books for Children
New York

First published in the United Kingdom by Egmont Books Limited, London
Text and illustrations copyright © 2004 by Knife and Packer
Volo® is a registered trademark of Disney Enterprises, Inc.

Printed in the United States of America
First U.S. edition, 2005
1 3 5 7 9 10 8 6 4 2

This book is set in 12/16 Excelsior.

ISBN 0-7868-5512-6

Visit www.hyperionbooksforchildren.com

CONTENTS

CLIFF THORNHILL
TV'S WORST WEATHERMAN

PUDDLES
THE ONLY WEATHERDOG ON TV

CAPTAIN FACT
THE WORLD'S FIRST INFORMATION SUPERHERO

KNOWLEDGE
CAPTAIN FACT'S FAITHFUL SIDEKICK

LUCY
HEAD OF MAKEUP AND
CLIFF'S BEST FRIEND

THE BOSS
HE'S SCARY!

PROFESSOR MINUSCULE
HEAD OF THE FACT CAVE AND
HE BRAINS BEHIND THE MISSIONS

FACTORELLA
PROFESSOR MINUSCULE'S
DAUGHTER AND ALL-AROUND
WHIZ KID

CHAPTER 1
DINO-DISASTER

TV's worst weatherman, Cliff Thornhill, and his sidekick, Puddles the dog, were in their office playing their favorite computer game, Dinosaur Attack III.

"This is great," said Cliff. "I love it when the Boss goes on vacation!"

"I keep being eaten by the Tyrannosaurus rex," Puddles said. "Those dinosaurs are scary!"

"It's not the dinosaurs, it's you," said Cliff. "Let me try."

Just as Cliff picked up the controls, there was a loud knock at the door.

Before Cliff could even say "come in," the door burst open. There stood the Boss—and he wasn't in a good mood. . . .

"Thornhill! You're useless!" he shouted. "You predicted two weeks of sunshine."

"Did it rain?" asked Cliff sheepishly.

"Rain? It rained so much I had to use a snorkel just to get to my bedroom! In fact, it was so awful that I decided to come back early."

"It's great to have you back," mumbled Cliff as the Boss slammed the door.

"Phew!" said Puddles, who only spoke when there was no one else around. "Lucky he didn't see the computer game."

Just then, there was another knock at the door. "HIDE!" shouted Cliff. He and Puddles ducked under the desk.

"Cliff? Puddles? What are you doing under the desk?" Luckily, it wasn't the Boss. It was Lucy, Cliff's friend from the Makeup department.

Cliff and Puddles emerged from underneath the desk.

"Have you seen the news? A dinosaur egg hatched at the museum!" said Lucy.

"That's amazing—a real live dinosaur!" said Cliff. "But wait—dinosaurs are extinct."

"Yes, and this little dinosaur will be, too, without her mother," Lucy said sadly.

"Too bad," said Puddles as soon as Lucy left the office. "But come on, let's get back to Dinosaur Attack III—this time I'm going to beat those dinosaurs."

"Forget computer-game dinosaurs, Puddles," said Cliff. "It's time you met a real dinosaur! This is a—"

"Not so fast!" interrupted Puddles. "I want to say it . . ."

"Well, then, get going!" said Cliff.

Puddles coughed theatrically. "This is a mission for Captain Fact!"

Then he jumped off his chair and yanked on a nearby lever to reveal the pole that led to the Fact Cave. . . .

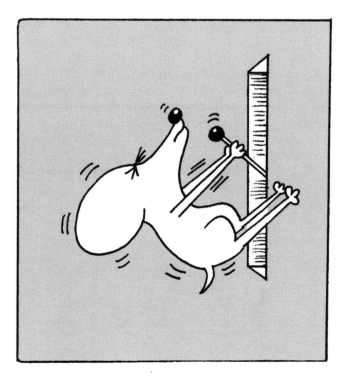

FACT CAVE

"We've got to save that dinosaur!" said Captain Fact as they ran down the hall to the Fact Cave Nerve Center. . . .

"I'm not sure I really want to meet a real live dinosaur," said Knowledge.

"Don't worry, I'm sure the dino will like you," said Captain Fact.

"Why can't the museum
just take the baby dinosaur to the
zoo?" asked Knowledge. "They'd be able
to look after her. They look after lizards and
crocodiles all the time, don't they?"

"You need some baby-
dinosaur facts," said
Captain Fact, as his nose
began to tremble and he
prepared for a . . .

"Knowledge, it looks like we're going to have to reunite the baby dinosaur with her mother," said Captain Fact as he opened the door of the Nerve Center.

"Great!" said Knowledge. "But how are we going to go back millions of years to find the dinosaurs?"

CHAPTER 2

BLAST BACK

"**C**aptain Fact and Knowledge, there you are!" said Professor Minuscule, emerging from behind a large box. Professor Minuscule was the world's shortest genius and the head of the Fact Cave.

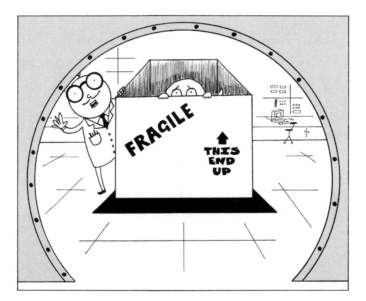

"Aaaaagh!" screamed Knowledge. He leaped into Captain Fact's arms. "There's a huge green cat in that box!"

"That's not a cat," said Professor Minuscule quickly. "That's Tricky, the baby triceratops. Tricky, this is Captain Fact and Knowledge. They're going to bring you back to your mother."

"Eeek," said Tricky, who could only speak in baby-dinosaur squeaks.

"Does she bite?" Knowledge asked nervously.

"Don't be silly, Knowledge," said Captain Fact. "**KER-FACT!** Triceratops are herbivores. That means they eat only plants. You know, grass, leaves, flowers . . ."

"That's disgusting," said Knowledge.

"There's no time to waste," Minuscule said, interrupting the conversation. "The museum has entrusted me with Tricky, and you're her only hope.

"Now, I've invented the world's first fully functioning time machine. It will take you and Tricky back to the time of the dinosaurs," Minuscule said.

"That's amazing!" said Captain Fact.

"You built a time machine that actually works?" he continued.

"Well . . . most of the time . . ." Professor Minuscule said softly.

"Most of the time? What do you mean, most of the time?" asked Captain Fact anxiously.

Just then, Factorella bounced in, and Minuscule breathed a sigh of relief.

"When do we go, Dad?" Factorella asked excitedly. "I've been reading all about dinosaurs, and I can't wait to see them!"

"You know you're too young to go on missions, Factorella," sighed Professor Minuscule. "You've still got years of training ahead of you before you can become a superhero. Now, what have you learned about dinosaurs?"

Factorella looked sad, but turned to Factotum, the Fact Cave's supercomputer.

JURASSIC PERIOD:
208–144 MILLION YEARS AGO—
THIS TIME PERIOD WAS WET AND WARM, WITH HUGE FLOODS. LOTS OF PLANTS GREW, WHICH MEANT THAT MASSIVE PLANT-EATING DINOSAURS EVOLVED. THE FIRST BIRDS APPEARED.

CRETACEOUS PERIOD:
144–65 MILLION YEARS AGO—
DURING THIS PERIOD, THERE WAS EXPLOSIVE GROWTH IN LIFE, AND THERE WERE LOTS OF DINOSAURS. THE FIRST SNAKES, MODERN MAMMALS, AND FLOWERING PLANTS APPEARED.

"What's wrong, Knowledge? You look pale," said Captain Fact.

"I have the feeling we're going to bump into a lot of these dinosaurs," Knowledge whined.

Minuscule ignored Knowledge. "I'd like to show you something special. . . ." He pressed a large red button on the remote-control device he was holding, and the floor and walls began to shudder.

"This is my finest creation yet: the Past-Blaster 3000."

In front of them was a gleaming time machine.

Captain Fact, Knowledge, and Tricky approached the machine as Factorella looked on enviously.

"You said it worked *most* of the time?" asked Captain Fact. "What, exactly, did you mean by that?"

"Well, it does occasionally miss the intended time period," replied Minuscule as he pushed them in the direction of the time machine. "But no need to worry. Everything will be fine. Now, please take your seats."

"'Occasionally miss the intended time period'?" repeated Captain Fact anxiously. "That means we could end up anywhere!"

But just then, the engines started up, and it became too noisy for Professor Minuscule to hear him. . . .

SECRET FACT!

(Shhh! Don't tell!)

OW DID CAPTAIN FACT MEET KNOWLEDGE?

CHAPTER 3

UG!

As the Past-Blaster 3000 flew back in time, the three intrepid time travelers were shaken and tossed all around the inside of the machine.

Suddenly, the time machine shuddered to a halt.

"Wow, that was some ride!" gasped Captain Fact, adjusting the mask over his eyes.

"It felt like being in a giant washing machine," panted Knowledge. "I feel like a pair of soggy socks."

"Professor Minuscule warned us that this machine sometimes makes mistakes," said Captain Fact as he looked around. Before he could figure out what time period they had landed in, Tricky started making strange squeaks.

"Maybe she's trying to tell us something," said Knowledge.

Suddenly, there was a loud cracking noise. . . .

"There's a dinosaur trying to climb on board!" screamed Knowledge.

"That's not a dinosaur, Knowledge. That's a woolly mammoth!" said Captain Fact worriedly. "Run!" he cried as he grabbed Tricky, and they all jumped out of the time machine and made a dash for it.

"Let's hide in this cave," suggested Knowledge.

"**KER-FACT!** We haven't gone back far enough in time," said Captain Fact, slightly out of breath. "Woolly mammoths lived in the Quaternary period." And with that, his elbow began to itch as he felt the beginnings of another . . .

"Why don't we wait here until the mammoths have moved on?" said Captain Fact as he peered out of the entrance to the cave.

"I'm starving," said Knowledge. "Where do you get dog biscuits around here? Do you think I should ask that man over there?"

"Man?" Captain Fact said in shock. He spun around. Right behind them stood a caveman.

"Ug!" said the caveman, who had never met a superhero before.

"Ug!" replied Captain Fact, who had never met a caveman before.

Luckily for the superheroes, the caveman seemed friendly and held out an enormous chunk of charred woolly-rhino meat.

"That's disgusting!" said Knowledge.

"Er . . . thank you. That's very nice of you," said Captain Fact, trying to be polite to the caveman. "I'll put it in my bag for later."

"You don't have any woolly rhino–flavored dog biscuits, do you?" asked Knowledge.

"Don't be ridiculous, Knowledge," said Captain Fact, as his nose began to twitch and he prepared himself for another . . .

Captain Fact and Knowledge were on a mission, though, so they couldn't hang out with the caveman for long.

"Looks like the mammoths have gone," said Captain Fact. "Let's get back to the time machine."

"Good-bye, Caveman," said Captain Fact.

"Ug," said the caveman.

Keeping a lookout for any more mammoths, they returned to the Past-Blaster 3000.

Once again the three time travelers took their seats and took off, hoping to reach the right time period.

CHAPTER 4
TRIASSIC TERROR

As the time machine whirred and spun, a familiar voice came through over the intercom.

"Professor Minuscule here—*crackle*—sorry about that detour—*pop*—but I should warn you, I'm still having some technical difficulties with the time machine—*fizz* . . ."

Before Captain Fact could respond, the Past-Blaster 3000 ground to a screeching halt.

"Let's hope this is the right time target," said Captain Fact.

They looked out over a large lagoon surrounded by odd-looking palm trees.

"I don't care if this *is* the wrong time period. Check out the beach!" said Knowledge excitedly. "Let's go for a swim!"

The time travelers stepped out of the Past-Blaster 3000, and Knowledge headed straight for the beach.

As Knowledge jumped into the inviting water and started splashing around, Tricky started making the strange squeaking noise again.

"I don't think that that is a good idea," said Captain Fact as Knowledge played in the warm water.

"What do you mean? It's beautiful in here!" said Knowledge.

"I think Tricky's squeaks are a warning," said Captain Fact. And then his jaw dropped, and he screamed, "Watch out behind you, Knowledge!"

"I've never seen you move that fast," said Captain Fact after Knowledge had leaped out of the water.

"What *was* that thing?" asked Knowledge.

"I think that was a nothosaur," said Captain Fact, "which means we might be in the Triassic period!"

"Well," said Knowledge, looking on the bright side, "at least we're safe up in these palm trees."

But just then, there was a rustle in the bushes.

43

"Don't be so sure we're safe. Those are lagosuchus," said Captain Fact as a group of skinny, long-legged reptiles ran toward them. "They might be only fifteen inches long, but I don't like the look of them."

"Throw them the woolly-rhino meat that the caveman gave us," said Knowledge.

"**KER-FACT!** We've gone back 60 million years too far!" said Captain Fact as he tossed the ravenous reptiles the meaty bone. "While they're having lunch, let's get to the Past-Blaster 3000."

"This time-travel thing is even scarier than I thought!" wheezed Knowledge as they beat a hasty retreat from the Triassic period. "How did other dinosaurs survive with all these predators around?"

"Dinosaurs had all kinds of tricks to stay alive," said Captain Fact as his earlobes began to wobble, and he felt the start of a . . .

FACT

DINO CARDS

NAME:
ANKYLOSAURUS

SPECIAL WEAPON:
ARMOR-PLATED SKIN AND
SPIKED BACK

POWER:
AN UNPLEASANT MOUTHFUL
FOR ANY PREDATOR

TERROR RATING:
★★★★★
CRUNCHY ON
THE OUTSIDE!

NAME:
IGUANODON

SPECIAL WEAPON:
SPIKED THUMB

POWER:
CLAWING—IDEAL FOR
SELF-DEFENSE

TERROR RATING:
★★★★★
THUMBS UP TO
IGUANODON!

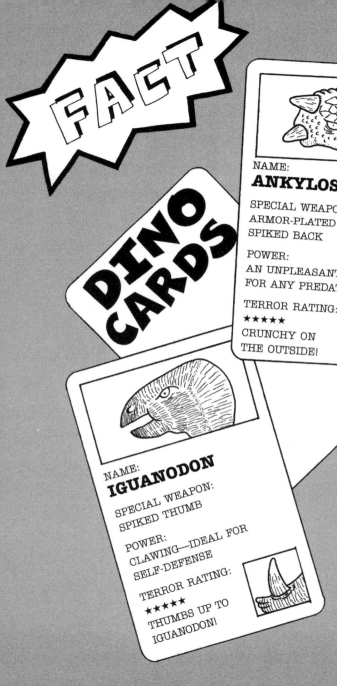

NAME:
DEINONYCHUS

SPECIAL WEAPON:
GIANT CLAW ON SECOND TOE

POWER:
GOOD FOR HUNTING AND
FISHING, AS WELL AS
SLASHING AND
RIPPING!

TERROR RATING:
★★★
YIKK!

NAME:
PARASAUROLOPHUS

SPECIAL WEAPON:
HOLLOW SKULL CREST CAN
MAKE LOUD NOISE

POWER:
CAN ALERT HERD AND SCARE
OFF PREDATORS

HONK!

TERROR RATING:
★★★
EARPLUGS IN!

NAME:
STEGOSAURUS

SPECIAL WEAPON:
CLUBBED TAIL

POWER:
TAIL CAN BE USED LIKE A
WHIP—SOME EVEN HAVE
SPIKES!

TERROR RATING:
★★★
OUCH!

ATTACK!!!

As they sat in the Past-Blaster 3000 getting ready to take off, something strange started happening: they felt themselves begin to rise up.

"What's going on?" asked Knowledge. "It feels like we're in an elevator."

"Don't worry," said Captain Fact, looking down. "It's a tanystropheus. **KER-FACT!** They only eat fish, and their necks are longer than their bodies."

"Phew," said Knowledge. "For a second, I thought we were going to be lunch."

CHAPTER 5
FLIGHT FRIGHT

"**K**nowledge, no!" shouted Captain Fact.
Knowledge had slipped and landed on
the control panel. "You hit fast
forwaaaaaaaaaaaaaaaaaaaaaaaard . . ."

Millions of years had spun by before the
Past-Blaster 3000 finally screeched to a
halt. Captain Fact was about to yell at
Knowledge when a voice crackled over the
intercom.

"Professor Minuscule here—*pop*— Thanks to Knowledge's bottom, you're in the Jurassic period—*crackle*—little 'accident,' 100 million years off target— *fizz*—I'm going to have to recalibrate the navigation—*whirr*—whatever you do— *crackle*—do not leave the time machine."

"That's too bad," said Knowledge. "It looks nice and warm out there. Look at all those trees and plants."

"Here we go—*crackle*—prepare to blast off. . . ."

"Stop!" shouted Captain Fact.

"Professor Minuscule, Tricky seems to have left the time machine," Captain Fact looked panicked. "We're going to have to take a closer look at the Jurassic period. We'll be back as soon as we can."

Captain Fact and Knowledge jumped out of the Past-Blaster 3000 and started searching for Tricky.

They looked all through the dense Jurassic undergrowth. They were just about to give up when they heard a familiar squeak.

"It's Tricky!" said Captain Fact. He had spotted their missing triceratops baby.

"Hey, why is it getting dark all of a sudden?" asked Knowledge. "That's the biggest cloud I've ever seen."

"I don't think that's a cloud, Knowledge," said Captain Fact, as his knees began to knock and he felt the start of another . . .

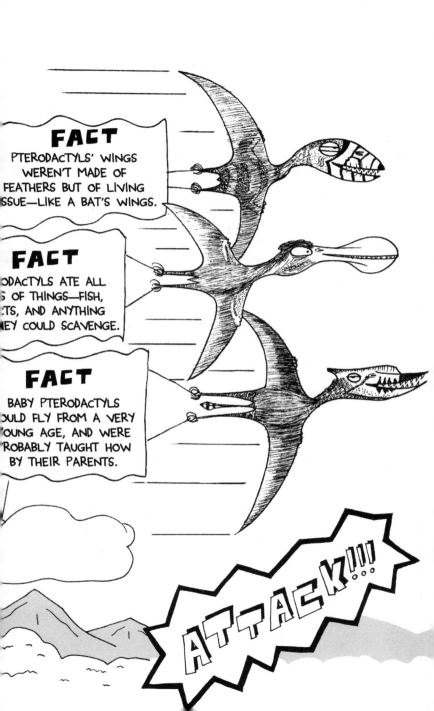

Captain Fact had barely finished having his Fact Attack when they were all swept off the ground by a flock of very angry pterodactyls.

"Hang on tight, we're landing!" warned Captain Fact.

"Phew," said Knowledge. "That's a relief. And look, little baby pterodactyls. They're so cute!"

"Cute, but hungry," said Captain Fact. "And I think we're what's for dinner!"

And with that, the pterodactyls dropped Captain Fact, Knowledge, and Tricky in among the hungry babies.

"Hello there, little pterodactyls," said Knowledge nervously. "You don't want to eat us, do you? Look, I'm horrible and furry, and he's wearing tights—not tasty."

"**KER-FACT!** Pterodactyls' young are fed on regurgitated and partly digested food," said Captain Fact.

"That's really gross," said Knowledge.

"No kidding," said Captain Fact. "So before their parents decide to gobble us up and spit us out, let's get out of here. I've got a plan. . . ."

"You're going to have to trust me on this one, Knowledge," said Captain Fact as he grabbed a large discarded fish tail from the nest.

"You know I'm afraid of heights," said Knowledge as Tricky looked gingerly over the edge of the cliff.

"Sorry, Knowledge, but it's jump or be regurgitated," said Captain Fact.

They all grabbed hold of the tail and jumped.

CHAPTER 6
JURASSIC JAWS

"**M**uch as I like your improvised-glider idea," said Knowledge, "I have one little question. Where are we going to land?"

"Well, actually . . . I hadn't thought of that," Captain Fact answered. They were miles from shore and heading straight out to sea.

"After meeting that nothosaur in the Triassic period, I'm not up for any more prehistoric swimming," said Knowledge anxiously.

"Well, it looks like you won't have to," said Captain Fact. "There's an island! We're saved!"

Captain Fact, Knowledge, and Tricky glided down onto the surface of a small, round island.

"Strange," said Captain Fact, "it seemed like the island just appeared. . . ."

". . . And it feels like it's moving," said Knowledge, who smelled something fishy.

"You're right, Knowledge. We appear to be floating," Captain Fact said nervously. He looked down at the churning water. "And I wonder if all prehistoric islands had four legs and a heaaaaaaaaaaad!

"I think we may have landed on the back of some sort of turtle," continued Captain Fact. "**KER-FACT!** Prehistoric turtles like the archelon could be up to thirteen feet long and weigh up to three tons!"

"At least we're heading in the right direction," said Knowledge. "Nothing can possibly go wrong now."

Just then, Tricky made a squeaking sound. . . .

"I've got a bad feeling about this . . ." said Captain Fact.

A huge, gaping mouth suddenly appeared out of the sea.

"What is *that*?" screamed Knowledge.

"**KER-FACT!** It's a liopleurodon, one of the most terrifying marine predators of all time. And turtles happened to be one of his favorite snacks," replied Captain Fact.

"This doesn't look good," said Knowledge.

"I think we're going to have to call Professor Minuscule!" And with that, he pressed the emergency button on his Fact Watch.

Just as the jaws of the liopleurodon were about to close on the turtle, Factorella appeared in her own time machine and saved them.

"You're lucky Dad had already sent me back to the Jurrassic era," said Factorella. "I've been repairing the Past-Blaster 3000. Isn't it great here? Dinosaurs everywhere! By the way, how did that dent get on the control panel? Looks like one of you sat on it or something."

"Um, really?" Knowledge said, trying to look innocent.

"Well, it's repaired now," said Factorella. "I'll wait until you're on dry land. Then I've got to blast back to the Fact Cave—Dad's baking cookies, and I'll be in trouble if I'm not back while they're still warm. Good luck with the rest of the mission!"

As Factorella's time machine groaned under the pressure of the liopleurodon's jaws, the turtle swam in the direction of shore.

"To think I used to be scared of sharks," said Knowledge. "I wonder what else is out there?"

"Funny you should ask that," replied Captain Fact, as his ears began to twitch and he felt the start of another . . .

At last, they reached the shore. In the distance they saw a flash of light as Factorella took off.

"Well, let's get going," said Captain Fact as he began walking away from the archelon.

CHAPTER 7
LAVA PALAVER

"**C**heck out the Past-Blaster 3000! It's fixed." Knowledge said as they got closer to the polished and shiny time machine.

"Now that Factorella's taken care of it, we should have no problem getting to the Cretaceous period," said Captain Fact as he started the machine up. "You'll be back with your mom in no time, Tricky."

"Look! Factorella left me some dog treats. Beef-flavored! My favorite!" said Knowledge.

With a flourish, Captain Fact pressed the takeoff button. Once again, they were traveling through time.

A short while later they shuddered to a stop, and the intercom sprang to life.

"*Fizz*—Welcome to the Cretaceous period—*crackle*—at last!" announced Professor Minuscule. "Now all you've got to—*fizz*—do is find Tricky's mother."

"Wow! It's beautiful here," said Knowledge as he looked around the lush landscape.

"Now's not the time to check out the view, Knowledge," said Captain Fact. "We're finally in the right time period, and we've got to get Tricky home."

Just then the ground began to shake.

"Is your stomach rumbling?" asked
Knowledge.

"No! It's a volcano!" shouted
Captain Fact.

RUN!

All around them dinosaurs were running away from the advancing lava.

"We're going to be swept away!" panted Knowledge as he ran next to Captain Fact.

"Let's get on the back of this big diplodocus," said Captain Fact.

"How are we going to do that? That dinosaur is gigantic!" screeched Knowledge.

"**KER-FACT!** Diplodocuses are over

sixteen feet tall!" said Captain Fact.

Grabbing Tricky, Captain Fact and Knowledge ran up the tail of the diplodocus.

"This is kind of weird," said Knowledge. "We've spent most of this mission running away from dinosaurs, and now we're running up one!"

"Oh, don't worry," said Captain Fact as his toes began to tremble, and he felt the rumblings of another . . .

"Those are some amazing facts!" said Knowledge. "But none of those creatures is Tricky's mother."

"Good point, Knowledge," said Captain Fact. "We need to find her."

CHAPTER 8
CRETACEOUS CRITTERS

When they had gotten safely away from the volcano, they slid off the back of the diplodocus.

"Can't we look up *Triceratops* in the phone book?" asked Knowledge.

"Knowledge! Don't be silly! We're going to have to use the Power of Fact," said Captain Fact. "**KER-FACT!** Triceratops moved around in huge herds."

"So we're looking for a large group of enormous dinosaurs," said Knowledge. In the distance, there was a strange knocking noise. "Would they be playing baseball?"

"I don't think so," said Captain Fact. "But maybe we should investigate."

They walked into a clearing, where they saw the strangest-looking dinosaurs yet.

"What are those?" asked Knowledge. "They look like crazed wrestlers."

"**KER-FACT!** Knowledge, those are pachycephalosaurs, the biggest of the 'boneheads,'" said Captain Fact. "That knocking noise is caused when they ram their heads together—it's their way of fighting *and* frightening off enemies."

"Ouch!" said Knowledge. "Well, I hope they have plenty of aspirin."

"Don't worry about them. Their skulls are up to nine inches thick!" said Captain Fact.

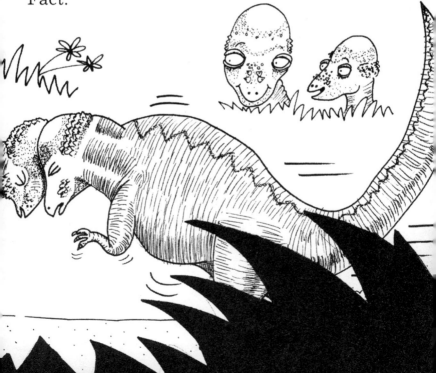

"While that is very interesting," said Knowledge, "it's still not helping us find Tricky's mother."

"Actually, you're wrong, Knowledge," said Captain Fact. "**KER-FACT!** Pachycephalosaurs are herbivores, just like the triceratops, so we're looking in the right place."

"I love herbivores," said Knowledge fondly. "They carry you around, make silly noises, and best of all, they don't try to eat you."

Just then, Captain Fact noticed that the pachycephalosaurs had stopped bashing their heads into one another and were nervously sniffing the air. Tricky had started squeaking again.

"There's only one problem with herbivores, Knowledge," said Captain Fact. "They attract carnivores!"

"Like that one over there with the funny little arms?" asked Knowledge.

"Don't forget the great big teeth—it's a Tyrannosaurus rex!" shouted Captain Fact.

As they ran away, his forehead began to throb, and he felt the start of another . . .

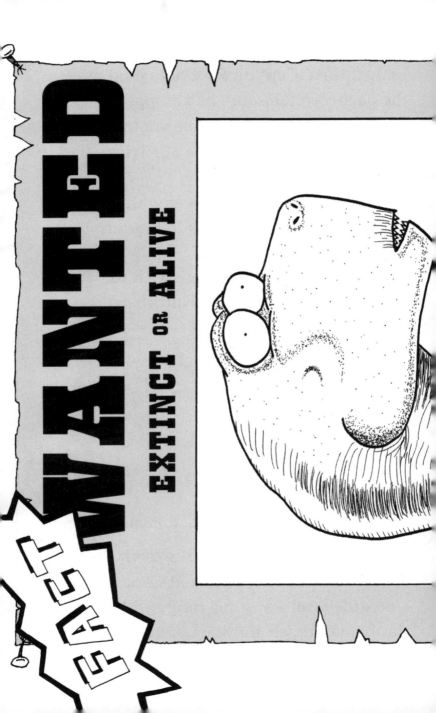

TYRANNOSAURUS REX

FACT: *TYRANNOSAURUS REX MEANS "KING OF THE TYRANT LIZARDS."*

FACT: A T. REX'S STRIDE WAS ALMOST SEVENTEEN FEET LONG—MORE THAN MOST PEOPLE CAN LONG-JUMP!

FACT: A T. REX'S HANDS HAD TWO FINGERS THAT WEREN'T MUCH BIGGER THAN YOURS!

FACT: ONE OF THE MOST FAMOUS T. REX FOSSILS IS ALMOST TWENTY FEET HIGH. THE CREATURE WOULD HAVE WEIGHED UP TO SEVEN TONS. IT'S IN THE FIELD MUSEUM IN CHICAGO AND IS NICKNAMED "SUE."

FACT: A T. REX PROBABLY COULDN'T RUN VERY FAST.

FACT: BUT T. REX WASN'T THE BIGGEST PREDATORY DINOSAUR: THAT WAS *GIGANTOSAURUS*, WHOSE SKULL WAS THE SIZE OF A HUMAN BEING.

Suddenly, Captain Fact and Knowledge found themselves backed into a corner. Things were looking bleak.

"This is just like Dinosaur Attack III," whispered Knowledge.

"So, what happens now?" asked Captain Fact.

"G—g—game over," stuttered Knowledge.

CHAPTER 9
SNAP-HAPPY

Suddenly, the earth began to rumble, and a huge cloud of dust could be seen in the distance. It was headed straight for them.

"What now?" asked Knowledge. "Don't tell me his brothers and sisters have been invited to the superhero meal as well."

The Tyrannosaurus rex stopped in its tracks.

"It's a herd of triceratops! We're saved!" shouted Captain Fact, as his toes began to curl and he was launched into another . . .

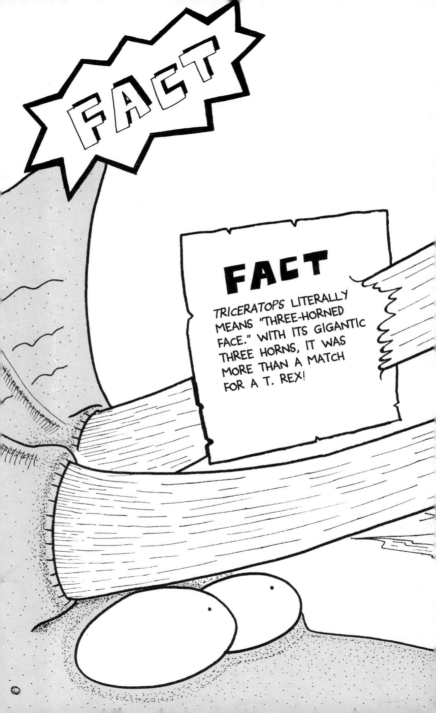

The Tyrannosaurus rex roared once defiantly, then pounded away as fast as its legs could carry it.

"Scaredy-cat!" shouted Knowledge. "When the going gets tough . . ."

"Not so fast, Knowledge," warned Captain Fact. "One of the triceratops is charging straight at us!"

"Well, it's been great knowing you, Captain. And Tricky, I'm sorry we couldn't help you find your mother," said Knowledge.

"Not even the Power of Fact can get us out of this one," said Captain Fact grimly.

Captain Fact and Knowledge braced
themselves for the inevitable collision. But
at the last second, the triceratops screeched
to a halt.

"Mama!" said Tricky.

"It's Tricky's mother," said Knowledge.
"I can't believe we actually found her!"
"Aren't they sweet?" asked Captain Fact
as he prepared the Fact Watch camera.

"Very cute, but I'm starving," said Knowledge. "When do we get to go home?"

"Just as soon as I've taken a picture for Professor Minuscule," replied Captain Fact.

After Captain Fact had taken his photo, Tricky invited them to hop onto her mom's back.

"I think she's offering us a ride back to the time machine," said Captain Fact as he jumped aboard.

And so they set out across the prehistoric landscape for the final time.

CHAPTER 10

ND NOW, THE WEATHER . . .

Soon they were safely back at the Past–Blaster 3000.

Captain Fact gave Tricky a hug. "I'm going to miss you, Tricky, but it's best that you're back with your mother."

"You can have my last dog biscuit," said Knowledge, handing over a slightly chewed doggy treat. Then he gave Tricky a huge hug.

They stepped aboard the time machine.

"We'd better slip out of our superhero outfits," said Captain Fact. "We're heading straight to the TV studio for the evening forecast."

And with a final wave, they blasted off.

After a lot of shuddering and shaking, the Past-Blaster 3000 ground to a halt.

"Welcome back to the twenty-first century—*fizz*," said Professor Minuscule over the intercom. "I've got some good news and some bad news. The good news is you're in the right time period—*crackle*—the bad news is . . ."

"We're in the Boss's office!" screamed Captain Fact. "Professor Minuscule, get rid of the time machine at once! Knowledge, let's get out of here!"

WHOOSH

As the Past-Blaster 3000 vanished, the Boss rubbed his eyes in stunned disbelief.

"I must be losing it. I could have sworn I just saw Thornhill and Puddles climbing out of a time machine," the Boss mumbled. "I'm just tired. I need the day off."

SLAM!

As the Boss booked himself another vacation, Cliff and Puddles ran in to the Makeup department.

"Cliff and Puddles! Where have you been?" asked Lucy. "I've been looking everywhere for you. Do you remember that baby dinosaur?"

"Yes," said Cliff.

"Well, Captain Fact and Knowledge managed to get her back to her mother!" said Lucy, holding up the evening paper. "I think Captain Fact looks very handsome in this picture. I'd love to go out with him!"

Cliff blushed bright red as he and Puddles stepped through the door into the TV studio.

With Tricky safely back with her mother in the Cretaceous period, Cliff Thornhill and Puddles were back to doing what they did worst—the weather.

Until the next crisis . . .

KNIFE & PACKER FACT!

IF KNIFE AND PACKER COULD INVITE ANY DINOSAUR TO DINNER, IT WOULD BE A *DIPLODOCUS*. HIS INCREDIBLY LONG NECK AND TAIL WOULD MAKE HIM FUN TO DRAW—AND HE WOULD EAT ALL THE VEGETABLES!